Coffee and Dreams

By JJ Caler

Coffee and Dreams

By J.J. Caler

Published by JJ Caler Publishing

THE GLOVE BOX

By J.J. Caler

Published by JJ Caler Publishing

Copyright © 2024 J.J. Caler

THE
GLOVE BOX

CHAPTER 1

Dennis Mercer hadn't planned on buying a car that morning. He'd meant to grab coffee, maybe answer a few client emails, and mentally prepare for the afternoon install he was already late on. But then he saw it—the 1964 Pontiac Tempest, hunkered on the corner of the used-car lot like some forgotten relic trying very hard not to look gorgeous.

It didn't succeed.

Even beneath the gray crust of road grime, even with a cardboard For Sale sign half-sliding down the windshield, the thing shimmered. That deep metallic blue peeked through like bruised starlight, and Dennis felt the weird, magnetic tug that normally only old cameras or vinyl players gave him.

He pulled in without thinking.

The lot itself looked like it had been assembled from leftover pieces of other lots—

a cracked asphalt surface, a sagging pop-up canopy, and a small prefab sales office that leaned slightly left like it was tired of its own excuses. A stray balloon drifted lazily at knee height. A hand-painted banner hung crookedly overhead:

BIG MIKE'S AUTO EMPORIUM — WE MAKE DEALS HAPPEN

Big Mike himself emerged as if summoned.

He was neither big nor, Dennis suspected, a Mike. He was wiry, gray-haired, and wore aviators even though the sky was overcast. His grin was sharp as a tin can lid.

"You like classics?" he said, not bothering with hello.

Dennis's mouth moved before his brain caught up. "I... yeah. I do."

"Well," Big Mike said, sweeping an arm toward the Tempest, "she just rolled in on trade last night. Guy needed to offload quick. Didn't even clean her out yet. Price reflects that."

It did reflect that. The sticker was low enough to be either a gift or a warning.

Dennis circled the car slowly, fingers grazing the fender. The metal was cool, solid. Real. The interior was a time capsule of sun-faded vinyl and cigarette ghosts. The dash was dusty but intact. The glove box—hinges a little loose—was the only thing that didn't seem original. Someone had replaced it. Recently.

He didn't think much of it.

"Wanna hear her run?" Mike asked.

Dennis nodded.

The engine turned over with a rough, throaty cough, but once settled, it rumbled like something confidently alive. Dennis didn't smile often in front of strangers, but the sound pulled one out of him.

"That's the face of a man who just bought a car," Mike declared.

Dennis exhaled. "I'd need to see the title."

"Aaand that's where things get interesting."

Of course it was.

Of course.

Mike retreated into the little office, rummaged the desktop, cursed softly, rummaged again. He returned scratching his head.

"Title's... missing."

"That's kind of important."

"I know, I know, I know," Mike said, waving his hand as though shooing away the concept of legality itself. "It was here last night. I'll find it. You can start the paperwork meanwhile."

Dennis folded his arms. "No title, no sale."

Mike chewed his lip, thinking. Then he snapped his fingers. "Check the glove box."

"The glove box?"

"Guy said he left something for the next owner. Maybe he left the title, too. People get sentimental about their classics."

Dennis shot him a look but climbed into the driver's seat. He braced himself for fast-food wrappers or a decades-old parking ticket. Instead, when he pulled the handle, the glove box dropped open with a click.

Inside was a single envelope.

No dust.

No fold marks.

No explanation.

Just **the title**, crisp as the day it had been printed.

He lifted it slowly.

The smell of ozone prickled the air.

"Huh," Dennis muttered. "Convenient."

Mike peered in from the window. "Told you!"

Half an hour later, the Tempest was his—papers signed, handshake given, keys cold and heavy in his palm.

Dennis slid behind the wheel, heart thudding with the stupid kind of joy he hadn't felt since he was ten and found a working Game Boy at a yard sale. He started the engine, eased out of the lot, and then—because he absolutely couldn't resist—floored it.

The Tempest leapt like it'd been waiting years for permission. Tires barked. Smoke curled behind him. Big Mike pumped a fist in the air like a man who appreciated a dramatic exit.

Dennis laughed out loud as the speedometer climbed.

He headed straight to the car wash. His new car deserved better than grime and neglect.

He pulled into a stall, grabbed the vacuum hose, patted his pockets—

—and froze.

He was a dollar short.

"Are you serious?" he muttered at himself.

He checked the seats. The floor. Under the mats. The ashtray. Nothing.

Then he sighed and reached toward the glove box again.

Maybe he just hadn't looked closely enough the first time.

The moment the door swung open, something clinked softly.

Inside sat a neat stack of quarters—

exactly the amount needed.

Dennis blinked.

"Well," he murmured. "That's... weird."

He grabbed the coins and shut the glove box firmly.

Behind him, the Tempest's dashboard lights flickered once.

Just once.

Like a wink.

CHAPTER 2

The quarters clinked as Dennis fed them into the vacuum machine, still glancing back toward the Tempest like it might vanish if he looked away too long. Cars like this didn't land in his price range. They didn't land in his life. Not unless something was wrong, or something was coming.

The machine roared to life.

Dennis ducked into the back seat, working the hose between the folds of stained upholstery. Dust spiraled through the air like old ghosts being evicted.

Every few minutes he caught himself glancing toward the glove box again.

Coins.

Exactly enough coins.

Not a penny more.

Even for a coincidence, it had felt... intentional.

He ignored the prickle running up his spine.

When the interior finally passed the "not embarrassing" threshold, Dennis drove home with the windows down to chase out the remaining funk. Accelerating sent a pleasant, low vibration through the steering wheel—the kind that made him think maybe he should name this car.

He'd never named a car before.

He barely kept plants alive.

But this—this was something different.

His apartment complex was unremarkable: faded brick, too many satellite dishes, a dumpster that always smelled faintly of damp cardboard. But as he eased the Tempest into a spot near Building C, Dennis felt a stripe of pride warm his chest.

He turned off the engine and sat quietly, savoring the moment.

Then he reached for the glove box again.

Just looking, he told himself.

Curiosity, nothing more.

It opened with that same smooth click.

The quarters were gone.

Instead, sitting in the center like it had been placed there with ceremony, was a brand-new microfiber detailing cloth. Folded perfectly. Deep blue.

Same shade as the car.

Dennis blinked. "Okay. Nope. No. Absolutely not."

He closed the glove box.

Opened it.

Closed it again.

Each time, the cloth remained.

He leaned back. The Tempest's interior felt smaller now, the air strangely still. "So," he whispered, as if talking to the car would help him understand it, "you… what? You provide stuff? Is that your thing?"

The car said nothing, of course, but the dash lights gave a gentle, ambient glow—not a flicker this time, but a steady heartbeat-like pulse.

Dennis forced out a breath. "I'm not going to make a big deal out of this," he said to nobody. "I'm tired. I need food. And sleep. And maybe a psych evaluation."

He grabbed the cloth anyway, because he absolutely was not above free detailing supplies.

Later that evening, Dennis cracked open a frozen dinner and flipped through emails. His sister Lily sent a picture of his niece, Abby, proudly holding a crooked papier-mâché dolphin. His landlord wanted rent—of course. And a client wanted "just a few small revisions," which meant at least four hours of unpaid work.

Dennis set the laptop aside and rubbed his eyes.

Maybe the Tempest had been a bad idea.

A cool breeze slipped in from the open window. Outside, the metallic blue car sat gleaming under the streetlamp.

He grabbed his keys and headed back down, unable to shake the magnet of it.

The interior smelled better now. Cleaner. Like vinyl and lemon detergent. He sat in the driver's seat and rested his hand on the wheel.

"What are you?" he murmured.

He ran his palm across the dash pad and then opened the glove box again.

Empty.

No cloth. No envelope. No quarters.

A curious, hollow feeling settled in him. "Okay. So maybe you don't work on command."

He shut it.

Then opened it.

This time, a small flashlight rolled forward with a polite tap against the back edge of the door.

Dennis startled. "Nope. Nope! No. This is too—"

A shout cut through the twilight.

Dennis snapped upright, turning toward the sound.

Another shout, the sharp crack of something hitting pavement.

It came from around the corner—the breezeway leading to Building B.

He scrambled out of the car and jogged toward the noise.

After just a few steps, he hesitated.

Turned back.

Grabbed the flashlight from the glove box.

He flicked it on, giving it a tap in his hand. The flashlight's beam was thin but determined, slicing through the dark. As he rounded the corner, he found the source of the commotion:

A bicycle lay twisted near the stairs.

A girl—six, maybe seven—sat beside it clutching her knee, tears streaking her cheeks.

She was wheezing.

Short, sharp, panicked bursts.

Dennis froze for half a second—long enough to recognize the unmistakable sound of an asthma attack.

"Hey," he said softly, crouching beside her. "Are you okay? Can you breathe?"

She shook her head, eyes wide and wild, one hand clawing weakly at the collar of her shirt.

"Where's your inhaler? Do you have one?"

She nodded, then pointed shakily toward the tall grass beyond the sidewalk. Her breaths were getting shorter, faster—her panic feeding the attack.

Dennis swept the flashlight beam across the grass. Nothing.

"Okay. Okay," he whispered, scanning again, pushing aside clumps of weeds. His heart hammered hard enough to drown out everything else.

The flashlight beam caught something pale blue deep in the grass—a plastic inhaler, the cap missing.

He grabbed it instantly.

His stomach turned.

"How..." he whispered.

But the girl let out a ragged breath, and reality returned.

"Got it!" He hurried back, kneeling in front of her. "Here—it's okay. I found it."

She tried to take it but her hands were trembling too hard.

"It's okay," he said softly. "I've got you." He steadied the inhaler, helped her bring it to her lips, watched her manage a shaky first puff.

Then another.

Gradually, the wheezing began to ease. Her shoulders sagged.

"You're okay," Dennis murmured, relief washing through him so intensely it left him dizzy. "Just breathe. You're okay."

She finally looked up at him—eyes still wet, but steady now. "Thank you," she whispered.

Dennis nodded, swallowing the tightness in his throat. "Anytime."

But as he walked her to her building—where a terrified mother rushed out to scoop her up—Dennis couldn't stop thinking about the sequence of events:

The flashlight he never owned.

The beam that had scanned the grass.

The inhaler that would've been impossible to find in darkness without it.

He knew coincidence when he saw it.

He also knew when something was not coincidence.

When he returned to the Tempest, he approached it like someone approaching a sleeping animal. Respectful. A little afraid.

He opened the glove box again.

Empty.

Completely, eerily empty.

"Okay," Dennis whispered, voice barely more than breath. "I don't know what you are. Or why you do what you do."

The dash lights gave a faint pulse—once, like a blink.

"But," he continued, "if you're going to keep doing this... you better not let me down."

CHAPTER 3

For months after the bicycle incident, Dennis checked the Tempest's glove box, but there was nothing. Every few days, without even realizing he was doing it, he'd open the door, check that it was still empty, and close it again. It was like the girl and inhaler had overdrawn on its supernatural account. He never placed anything inside it, not even the registration that technically belonged there. He kept that in the center console instead. He warned passengers not to touch it — not that anyone rode with him often.

He didn't know what spooked him more:

that something was in there when he needed it,

or that something was never in there when he didn't.

Months passed. The Tempest became his escape — Saturday wax sessions, late-night drives to nowhere, parking at the overlook when he couldn't sleep. A borderline ritual. The glove box, in its eerie stillness, became an unspoken part of the car's identity. It was a quiet pact between them: he didn't ask, and it didn't offer.

At least, not until he met her.

Her name was **Sadie**. He saw her at the counter inside a tiny hardware store in the city — the kind that still smelled of lumber and machine oil. He'd gone in for sandpaper, walked out with a smile he couldn't shake and a receipt he couldn't remember signing.

She was witty in the way people sometimes were when they weren't trying. A little quirky. The kind of girl who tucked a pencil behind her ear even when she didn't need it and apologized every time she laughed too hard, which only made her laugh harder.

By the time he'd reached the door she said, "If you ever get bored driving around in that Pontiac alone, you should take me for a drive."

He'd never mentioned the car. She'd simply *noticed*.

He blurted, "I could— I mean, yeah, I'd like that," and immediately regretted how much enthusiasm vibrated in his voice.

She tore a narrow strip from the end of an invoice pad she had with her and scribbled her number. "Don't lose it," she said playfully.

He promised he wouldn't.

And he lost it.

Not immediately. Not even that day. But later — when the sky cracked open in a sudden Texas downpour the way it always did in late summer — he sprinted across the grocery store parking lot, juggling the week's supply of mac and cheese, milk, and the world's largest bag of discount coffee.

He fumbled for his keys.

The tiny piece of paper with her number slipped free.

Rain hammered it flat to the asphalt.
And before he could notice it, a passing car sent a fan of water across the pavement, sweeping the tiny strip straight down the gutter and into the storm drain.

After driving home and getting his armload of "*groceries*" put away, he tore through his pockets — nothing except keys and disappointment. He ran outside and checked the car. Nothing. The seats. The floor mats. The ashtray. Nothing.

Finally, defeated, sweat dripping, breathless, he slumped across the Tempest's front bench seat and pressed his forehead to the steering wheel.

Then he saw the glove box.

"No..." he whispered. "No, no, no. I didn't lose it. I *lost* it, but I didn't lose it. You hear me? Not this. Not her."

He closed his eyes, took a breath, and pulled the latch.

There, impossibly dry, impossibly safe, lay the narrow strip of paper with Sadie's number written in blue ink and her imperfectly beautiful handwriting.

He didn't touch it for several seconds. Just stared at it.

The Tempests yawning glove box stared back in silence.

Finally, he took the slip, folded it carefully, and grinned despite himself.

"Fine," he said to the glove box. "But don't make a habit of this."

CHAPTER 4

He called her that night. She laughed when he told her how he'd nearly lost her number to a storm drain, but left out the glove box. He didn't want her thinking he was crazy, even though he was beginning to. "Well," she said, "it's a good thing the universe is rooting for you."

He didn't correct her.

They decided to meet halfway between town and the city where she was working that day. A small diner off the highway, famous for its pie and terrible for its décor. Neither cared. They were too busy talking over each other on the phone, already teasing, already connected in that strange electricity that happens when two people who should've met years earlier finally collide.

The sky threatened rain again. A dark belly of clouds

gathered along the horizon painting its warning. Dennis wasn't worried. He'd driven the Tempest through worse, and something about tonight felt untouchable, like nothing could ruin it.

He left early, wanting to arrive before she did. He liked the idea of her walking in and seeing him already there, waiting with nervous hands wrapped around a cup of coffee.

The rain began ten minutes into the drive. Heavy. Thick. The kind that blurred headlights into long, trembling smears of gold. About as useful as a matchstick for seeing the road.

The Tempest handled fine, but visibility was nearly gone. Then, too late to stop, he went past the diner. He flicked the wipers to high, squinting. Cars passed him with too much confidence. One in particular stood out—a silver AMC — shot by in a spray of water, hydroplaned briefly, corrected, and continued.

Then, in the rearview mirror, he saw it fishtail.

Saw the brake lights flash.

Saw the car veer sideways and disappear over the soft shoulder of the road.

"Shit—"

He braked hard, pulling off the highway. Hazard lights blinking. The rain pounded harder, flattening his hair to his forehead the moment he stepped out.

The ditch wasn't a ditch at all, but a ravine. The slope was steep, slick, more mud than earth. At the bottom, crumpled against a small boulder, was the silver Concorde. Its tail end was submerged in muddy water rushing down the normally dry channel like a newborn river.

He slid, half-fell, and caught himself on a clump of dying grass.

"Sadie!" he called before rational thought could intervene.

A face rose in the shattered driver's window — pale, soaked, terrified and moaning loudly.

It was her.

He reached the car, heart pounding wildly, and pried at the door. It didn't budge. The frame had twisted in the crash. Inside, Sadie winced, gasping as she tried to move. Her leg was at a wrong angle — badly wrong — pinned near the column.

"It hurts... Dennis, it hurts—"

"You're gonna be okay. I'm right here."

The water in the ditch rose a little higher, filling the back seat.

He had minutes at best.

He tried the seatbelt. Jammed. Tried to lift her. She screamed.

He needed something. Something to cut. To pry. To splint.

Something he didn't have.

The Tempest sat above him on the shoulder, hazard lights pulsing through the downpour like a heartbeat.

He looked at the car.

Looked at Sadie.

Looked at the rising water around him.

"Don't leave me," she whispered.

He squeezed her hand. "I'm coming right back. Hold on. Just—hold on."

Then he turned and clawed his way up the mud, slipping twice, cursing, praying.

At the top, drenched and shaking, he yanked open the Tempest's door and reached for the glove box.

"Come on," he begged. "Please."

He opened it.

A small folding saw stared back at him.

He swore at it. Swore hard.

"I CAN'T AMPUTATE! WHAT THE HELL DO YOU WANT FROM ME? THERE HAS TO BE ANOTHER WAY!"

He slammed the glove box shut. Opened it again.

A small hand axe appeared.

"No! I'm not— I can't— I'M NOT GOING TO DO THAT!"

But the water was rising. And Sadie was screaming now, panicking.

He grabbed the axe and ran.

CHAPTER 5

Rain sheeted sideways across the embankment, turning the entire slope into a living slide of mud. Dennis nearly lost his footing halfway down, but the axe in his grip acted like a counterweight, dragging him forward, pulling him toward Sadie and the half-submerged wreck.

"Sadie!" he shouted over the roar of rain and the fast-rising water that was swallowing the ruined car.

Her head lifted from the headrest, her hair plastered to her cheeks, her breaths sharp and ragged.

"Dennis— hurry— I can't— the water—"

"I'm here! I'm here!" he said, though he wasn't sure she could hear him over the storm.

The driver's side was angled downward into the runoff, the waterline rising past her back and shoulders now, soaking the seat. She tried to lift herself again and cried out. Her leg was obviously broken — a clean snap somewhere below the knee judging by the swelling and angle — and wedged between the pedals and the crumpled paneling.

He put a hand on her soaked, trembling shoulder and helped hold her head up out of the water. "Look at me, okay? I'm going to get you out of here." He leaned in and tried to release the seatbelt, but it was jammed. The buckle, crushed from the impact, refused to unlatch. Dennis wiped the rain from his eyes and tried again. It didn't budge.

Her eyes flicked to the axe in his hand and widened. "What... what is that for?"

He hadn't actually thought about what he was going to say to her. He'd just run with the thing the glove box gave him when he heard her screams.

"It's for... I mean—"

He swallowed. He couldn't tell her he thought the car wanted him to amputate her leg. That was insane.

"I'm going to use it to get you free," he said instead, which was at least half true.

He lifted the axe.

"What are you— Dennis!"

"Not you. The belt. Lean back."

He swung once — the blade sank halfway through the belt. Swing two — it snapped, the edges fraying. Sadie gasped as the tension holding her to the seat disappeared.

Water surged above her torso, splashing up into her face. The car's rear section shifted slightly deeper into the mud.

"Okay," he breathed. "Now your leg."

She gritted her teeth. "Dennis, I can't move it— it's stuck— I can't—"

"Don't move. Just let me look."

He wedged himself between the car and a boulder, water up to his hips now, and braced his shoulder under hers to lift her slightly. She screamed, but he kept lifting long enough to see the problem: the metal near her foot was folded inward, trapping her ankle and half her calf like a vise.

He would need leverage. He would need something strong enough to wedge between the panel and the brake pedal and pry outward.

The axe wasn't right for that. The saw wasn't right either.

He scanned the embankment.

Nothing but mud and weeds. Nothing but water and dirt and—

His eyes caught it: the lone mesquite tree about twenty yards away, thin and leafless, its branches surprisingly straight.

A splint.

He couldn't amputate — but he *could* stabilize.

"Okay, Sadie," he said, steadying himself. "I'm going to prop you up. Just for a second."

He looked around for something to lean her against while he worked. The passenger headrest was intact. He leaned in and grabbed it, pulled hard, and it popped free, the rods bending under his grip. It would work.

He lodged it behind her shoulders like a brace to keep her upright and above the rising waterline.

"You're okay," he repeated, although his own heart hammered too hard for him to be sure of anything. The water was moving downstream as fast as it was rising. They could both be swept away at any moment and bashed into the banks or some boulder or canyon wall downstream.

He scrambled out of the ditch. Mud sucked at his shoes. The cold rain stung his skin. He hauled himself toward the mesquite tree, using the axe handle like a climbing tool, sinking it into the embankment for grip.

By the time he reached the tree, his breath was ragged and his hands trembled. He raised the axe, swung twice, and a straight branch cracked free. He took another. And another, for good measure.

By the bottom of the slope, the branches were already slick with rain. He dropped to his knees beside her.

"I can't— Dennis—"

"You can. You *will*."

He braced her leg between his own, trying not to think about how pale she was getting, how her breaths were turning shallow.

First, the flesh and bone: two branches on either side of her leg, bound with strips of ripped fabric from his shirt, leaving him in a white t-shirt. He knotted them tight, apologizing every time she winced.

Next: the metal.

He slid the axe head next to the folded panel, using the handle as a lever. It didn't budge.

"Come on," he growled. "Come on!"

The water reached her chest and she struggled to keep her head up.

"Dennis!" she gasped, losing strength in her neck.

He repositioned the axe, braced one foot inside the car and one outside, and shoved with every ounce of strength he had.

The metal shifted.

Screamed.

And gave.

Her leg came free.

"Okay— okay, I've got you," he said, sliding his arms beneath her and lifting her from the sinking car.

She yelped in pain but clung to him, her fingers cold and shaking against his shoulder. He held her tight, feeling her weight, her breath on his neck, the rain soaking both of them until they felt indistinguishable from the storm itself.

He carried her weight, pulling her through the muddy water until they reached the muddy bank. She reached out and together they got her out of the water. Then Dennis clambered up beside her, slipping on his way as the drenched soil broke away in his grasp.

But now came the hard part.

The climb.

The mud was worse now—flooding from above, washing in rivulets around their feet. Dennis tested his footing. It slid instantly.

He jammed the axe into the ground like a climbing pick.

It held.

"That's it," he told himself. "That's how."

One step at a time, he hooked the axe into the earth, pulled them both upward, and then found a foothold. Repeat. Again. Again.

Halfway up, his foot slipped and they lurched. Sadie gasped, clinging tighter.

"I've got you. I SWEAR I've got you."

He swung the axe again, burying it in the earth with a wet thud, and used it to drag them upward another two feet.

Rain blurred everything. His muscles screamed. His arms shook. But he kept going, pulling Sadie up the embankment inch by grueling inch, until finally — finally — his hand closed over the lip of the concrete reinforcement at roadside shoulder.

With a last heave, he pulled them both onto the asphalt.

They collapsed beside the Tempest, breathing hard, Sadie half-leaning against his chest as he cradled her upright.

"You came back," she whispered.

"Of course I did."

She looked at the axe still clutched in his hand. "I thought... you were going to..."

"I know." He exhaled shakily. "So did I, for a second."

Her brow furrowed in confusion.

He opened the passenger door to help her inside the Tempest. The glove box still hung open, rain speckling the seat.

In the distance, sirens began to rise — faint, but approaching. Relief flashed across Sadie's expression, followed by exhaustion.

Dennis tipped his shoulders inside leaning close, holding her, rubbing her back to warm her.

She sat inside the Tempest, quiet and still, watching the rain streaking down its deep blue hood.

CHAPTER 6.

The hospital room was quiet except for the soft rhythm of machines and the occasional murmur of voices in the hallway. Sadie lay propped against pillows, her leg wrapped and stabilized in a bulky boot-like cast. Her hair was brushed now, her clothes clean, the storm long since passed. A warm evening glow filtered through the blinds.

Dennis stood at the foot of the bed, hands in his pockets, feeling both out of place and unable to leave. He'd been there when she was brought in. He'd been there when the doctors checked her pupils and palpated her ribs. He'd been there when she squeezed his hand so tightly, he thought she might break it.

He hadn't left because—well, he couldn't. Not after everything.

Sadie noticed his lingering silence.

"You okay over there?"

He blinked. "I... yeah. Just... thinking."

"You're allowed to sit, you know." She gestured toward the chair beside her bed.

"Oh. Right. Yeah."

He sat awkwardly, the vinyl creaking beneath him.

She smiled — tired, but kind. "You saved my life."

He shook his head. "I don't know. I just... kept moving."

"That's what saving someone is."

Dennis swallowed, glancing at his hands. They were still red and scraped from the climb. "You don't understand. I thought—when I first grabbed that axe—I thought

I was going to have to do something horrible."

Sadie tilted her head. "Like what?"

He hesitated. "Amputate."

Her eyebrows lifted. "Dennis—"

"I know," he said quickly. "I know how that sounds. But that car... that... You were trapped."

"I think," she said, choosing her words carefully, "that maybe the universe points you. Not to answers. Just... to possibilities."

He looked at her then — really looked. The bruises along her collarbone. The faint drying lines where tears had mixed with rain on her skin. The softness around her eyes when she watched him.

"You know, I was terrified," he said quietly. "More of losing you than the storm or the mud or the car or that metal... trap around your leg. But, sometimes, you don't have to know. You just have to start."'

"And you did," she said.

"And I did," he echoed.

They sat in silence for a moment, the hum of the room filling the space between them. Sadie's fingers drifted toward her lap, absently smoothing the blanket.

"Can I tell you something?" she murmured.

"Anything."

"When the car first skidded, I thought... that was it. I thought I'd never see you again. And then when I saw you running down that hill— a part of me believed I'd imagined it. But you came."

"I came," he said, voice thick.

"And you didn't hesitate."

"Oh, I hesitated," he admitted, with a shaky laugh. "I hesitated plenty."

"But your feet still kept going," Sadie said. "Sometimes that means more than bravery."

He didn't have an answer to that, so he let the words settle in the warm air between them.

After a long moment, she reached out, palm up. An invitation.

He stared at her hand — small, soft, healing — and placed his own in it. Her fingers curled around his like they had when she was half-conscious in the storm, but now they held without fear.

"How long are you staying?" he asked.

"Overnight for observation," she said. "Maybe two nights, depending. But... I'd like you to visit. If you want to."

"If I want to?" He huffed a laugh. "Sadie, I'll be sleeping right outside your door if they let me."

She smiled, and it lit her whole face, brighter than the evening sun slipping through the blinds.

"Your car's still outside," she said, eyes warm with amusement.

"Yeah. I should probably... you know... close the glove box at some point."

She laughed gently. "You left it open?"

"Felt like it was waiting to judge me."

"Well," she said softly, "maybe it's waiting for you to trust it."

He looked at her, searching her expression. *Did she know something?'.*

He exhaled, the tension easing out of his shoulders. "Yeah," he whispered. "Maybe."

The nurse knocked softly and entered with a chart. "Visiting hours are ending soon."

Sadie gave him a small, tired smile.

He rose, hesitated only a moment, then leaned down and pressed a gentle kiss to her forehead — light, uncertain, honest.

When he stepped out into hallway and looked out the window, the storm had passed. The parking lot glistened. The Tempest sat alone under a streetlamp, rain still dripping from its hood.

He went out and opened the door.

Sat inside.

The glove box hung open exactly as he'd left it, the dark interior empty now except for a few scattered flecks from the raindrops.

He placed one hand on the door.

"I get it," he whispered. "Not answers. Just possibilities."

And for the first time since the day he bought the car, he closed the glove box without fear.

Waking In A Midnight Dream

By J.J. Caler

Published by JJ Caler Publishing

WAKING
IN A
MIDNIGHT
DREAM

PROLOGUE

Sometimes a dream isn't a dream. You enter a world that is out of your control. You gather your senses only in time to be taken away again.

But there are rare occasions, for rarer people, that a dream is something more. An opportunity... Or a torment. A view into the sight of another. A moment in time that doesn't belong to you and the choices you make could change everything.

A dream is not a dream when it is a dream walk

CHAPTER 1

Like waking in a midnight dream, I became suddenly aware, sitting in a restaurant at a table next to a family. A husband and wife, with a teenage son and a small daughter. But my thoughts were drawn to the host of new pains in my body. My bones ached. I could feel the odd form of badly healed breaks in my right hand. I rubbed my hands and gave my neck a roll to loosen it up.

As the night went on, I became somewhat involved with the family, finding the daughter especially entertaining as she seemed to gravitate to me and pull me into the conversation. She seemed especially keen on my pancakes with strawberries and whipped cream, which, with the grace of a grandfather, I offered to her untouched. The waitress, apparently in tune with the situation, delivered a fresh batch to the table without a word, along with a much-needed warming of the coffees.

The mother, in her mid-thirties, had blonde hair and green eyes. Familiar, and oddly attractive. I quickly dismissed the thought, taking in her husband next to her. He seemed familiar too. Slightly older than her, with reddish-brown hair and brown eyes. Fairly fit, at least not overweight. When he stood, you could see he was about six feet tall.

She mentioned she was a nurse and had to be up early in the morning. There was a lot going on, and most of it was going to land on her desk. She was in charge of inventory, making sure they had what they needed, clearing it with customs and homeland security, and a half dozen other government entities that seemed to be on a need-to-know basis. Then finding out what would be available on the ground when they arrived so there was no unnecessary overlap.

The husband joined in once in a while, offering extra details along the way. Apparently, he was in the same line of work. I could see they were very much the happy couple. After a warm night of conversation and new friends, I left, and shortly after, the mother did too.

As I walked out the door of the restaurant, I saw an unfamiliar reflection in the glass. A man in his sixties, with a bit of a scruffy beard. Gray hair, thinning at the top. And a few scars around his right eye that evidenced a not-too-easy ride through life. I ran my hand up across my forehead. What is going on?

The mother was walking while looking through her purse for her keys and bumped into a hedge next to a driveway with large white curbs. Taken by surprise, she nearly tripped and fell over the edge of the curb. I, who was just in the street a few yards away, saw her and called over, "Are you okay?" I asked while walking back toward her.

She explained that she was just distracted. She worked for a group of doctors that traveled into disasters and war zones. Her time with her children was becoming too short.

I looked at her, feeling there was more to say, but only managed, "Yes, it is."

She looked down, finding her keys. "There they are. Wait... What?" But when she looked back up, I was gone. I could still see and hear her, though, as if from behind a veil. She shivered slightly, thinking about what I had said. "Yes, it is? What did he mean by that? That was kind of a creepy thing to say." She shrugged it off and found her car. As she walked away, she seemed to fade into the distance, leaving me alone in the twilight.

CHAPTER 2

I woke up...

My mind was bouncing around, trying to get my bearings. I was sitting on a bleacher in some kind of small half amphitheater with a cafe and tables and chairs down below and to my right. There were tables set out on a patio area, and the open front cafe showered a bit of light onto the paving stones.

Below and to the left was the stage. There was a TV camera, a crew, and a few small families filling the tables. The seats in the bleachers were only sparsely covered with spectators. It was mildly dark around the tables and the bleachers, with the stage being lit up for prime viewing.

Trying to figure out where I was, I was vaguely aware of what was going on around me. A boy was called up, and then a small girl. It was some kind of quiz show. Each kid would pick a word from a list, then the kids would pick a member of the audience to help them. They would whisper the word to the audience member, who would try to answer three questions with common expressions containing the secret word.

I tried to focus on the game and see if I could anchor myself and figure out how I got there, and who I was. My head kept spinning and my vision kept blurring away. I rubbed my arms that were tingling. I looked at my hands, now missing the broken bones and smoother. I felt my face and chin, looking for a scruffy beard that was not there.

The boy picked someone from one of the tables, and they went to the other side of the stage to a small sofa to brainstorm. The host of the show turned to the girl and showed her the list of words. Apparently, if you were watching at home, you would know she picked strawberry.

The host swung his arm around, pointing to the people off the stage, "Go and choose your helper. Choose carefully. You get one chance."

The small girl looked around and locked her eyes on me in the bleachers. She quickly sprinted for me. "You are the one. It's you." She grabbed my arm and tugged me onto my feet. Leaning toward me, she whispered, "Strawberry."

I got up and followed along down the stairs, where one of the cast members pointed to a small sitting area next to the main stage. A matching sofa on this side of the stage to complement the one the others had just sat down on.

"Strawberry," I thought. *"Expressions with strawberry in them."* My mind was still lost in a flood. *"Let me take you down, 'cause I'm going to..."* The melody rolled through my mind like an echo, and a chill went down my back.

"I don't know many things with strawberry," I tried to focus on the game. "Strawberry shortcake, is that considered an expression?" I kept digging through my thoughts.

It seemed like an hour had gone by, barely aware of what was going on outside my own mind. The boy had somehow gotten disqualified, and the small girl had won. I wouldn't even appear on the show, which was great at this point, with no strawberries.

I got up and looked around for the door. As I fumbled my way out, the girl's mother noticed me. She looked to her husband, "That nice man, he doesn't look well. I need to go make sure he is okay."

He smiled, "Of course you do. Don't worry, I got your back here," he pointed to the two children.

I stopped, resting against a hedge. Looking out across the buildings, I could make out the cone of a large mountain. I knew that mountain. It was Mount Hood. "The pavement was unusually wet for an evening in Portland," I thought, sarcastically. I leaned forward, holding my forehead, desperately trying to figure out what was going on. How did I get here?

From behind me, the girl's mother called to me, "Are you okay?"

I answered quietly, "I don't think I have long."

"Is there something I can do? Should I call you an ambulance?" She looked at me with deep caring eyes, "I am a nurse."

I lifted my head, "That's it, that's right," I whispered to myself.

I looked at her, "This is the second time."

"What do you mean?" she asked.

I said, "You were right here, looking for your keys, last night. That was the first time."

She grew anxious, not recognizing me, but recalling looking for her keys, and the elderly man who had eaten next to them. I pointed at the hedge and the wide white curbs. The chill grew in my back.

I looked at her, tears almost in my eyes, "It won't be worth it," I barely got out. Then I fell to my knees.

She got down on her knees beside me, now in a pleading voice, "What do you mean! What won't be worth it?"

I gasped for air, "I can't breathe." My mind scrambled, realizing that telling her anything else would be the end right there on the spot. But I had to tell her somehow. And every word seemed to suffocate me.

She grabbed my arms below my shoulders, "Please, what is it!"

Suddenly, memories flooded into my mind.

CHAPTER 3

I was walking through the makeshift hospital, holding a locked case, and paused next to a desk where a nurse was seated, going through pages of notes and orders. Her desk was decorated in neo-organized chaos with a small family photo as the centerpiece.

Her husband, herself, and two small children.

"I have to go make the supply purchase. Do you feel like taking a break and getting something to eat?" I asked her.

"Oh my God, do you see this mess here? All of this has to be organized, itemized, and numerated to turn into the government. I am never going to get this done." She threw herself back in her chair.

"Yes, that is just what I was thinking. So, you might as well get a bite to eat. And since it's Tuesday, it will be my treat."

She turned her head to me with half a laugh, "Well, it's definitely Thursday, but you're right."

We walked about a block and turned into a small cafe. We seated ourselves at a table and the coffee began to flow. Quickly glancing at the menu, she said, "Well, I know exactly what I want... strawberry shortcake."

I smiled, "Really, they have strawberry shortcake?"

She held up the menu with her finger locked on the menu item, "I sure hope so. Because now that I have seen this, I really want it." She sipped her coffee. "Before we left to come here, baby girl was on this funny little show where they picked a word, and she picked strawberry."

She smiled quietly as she remembered.

The quiet was shattered as a gunman started firing shots and yelling. The man went straight to our table. He was wearing a black mask and a trench coat, holding a pistol. The sound of screams and glass breaking filled the air as people ran for cover. I felt a fear and a rage as I realized what was happening.

"The case!" he yelled.

I looked back at the gunman. Thinking quickly, "If I were alone, it might be worth the fight, but I can't risk these people." I reached down toward the floor to get the case.

The gunman grabbed the nurse and yelled again, "The case! Now!"

I held out the case. The gunman grabbed it, then shoved the nurse, whom he had pulled out of her chair.

I jumped out of my chair to grab her before she could fall, when another shot rang out.

I could see the blood forming a pool on the front of her white smock.

"No!" I yelled, "No, no, no!"

She slowly slipped toward the floor, slowing her fall by grabbing the table.

I went to my knees, and held her hand as her body came to rest. "No...!" I shouted, my voice cracking.

I pulled her up, hugging her to my chest.

"It's okay. I hate strawberries." She whispered and she fell limp in my arms.

***

As the memory rush ended, I looked up at her and breathed out one last word. "Stay."

And I closed my eyes.

CHAPTER 4

"Good afternoon, ladies and gentlemen. This is your captain speaking. We have just landed at Houston, Texas for a brief stopover. We will be on the ground for approximately 45 minutes to refuel and allow new passengers to board. For those of you continuing on to São Luís, Brazil, we kindly ask that you remain seated and keep your seatbelts fastened until we are ready to depart. Feel free to stretch your legs and use the lavatories if needed, but please stay within the cabin. We appreciate your cooperation and thank you for flying with us today. We'll be back in the air shortly."

The plane had landed smoothly, and the gentle hum of the engines was a comforting background noise. I was awakened when the captain's voice crackled through the intercom. My shirt was drenched in sweat. Not from the heat; the cabin was cold, especially now.

My eyes opened to the inside of a commercial airliner. I could feel the vibration of the engines and a slight pressure in my ears. The air smelled like a mix of coffee and perfume. Looking forward, my waking eyes began to see the rows of seats and the tops of a few heads above the seat-backs.

I wiped the sweat from my forehead and eyes, trying to piece together what was going on and how I got on this plane. I'd been bouncing through realities and was no longer sure I was awake. I felt in my pocket and found the ticket. Then I remembered getting the ticket and boarding the plane.

Curved walls disappeared into a curved ceiling, broken every foot or so with small roundish windows, some with little covers slid closed over the glass. The pale off-white color was broken up by soft blues on the seat upholstery and the occasional open door on an overhead compartment.

I looked out the window to my right, trying to come into focus. The blue sky and clouds rolled past below, occasionally allowing a brief glimpse of the ocean. Then I looked to my left, and there she was. The mother from the cafe, the nurse from the hospital, the woman from the restaurant. She was standing there with a small bag and a pet carrier with a big furry cat inside.

A cold chill ran down my spine, and the hairs stood up on my arms. I remembered the pancakes, the quiz show, and the case. I remembered the word that haunted me. Strawberry. Had any of that happened? What did it mean? Was I getting a glimpse into the future, or was I just exhausted?

Maybe that was it, exhaustion. I had been fighting for months to get my passport straightened out. There were a few hiccups along the way. And then the company made me go through training again. As if I had forgotten the last few years, all of a sudden.

As she placed her small bag into the overhead compartment, she introduced herself as a nurse and said where she was heading. She worked for a group of doctors that traveled around the world, and she loved her job. She asked what I did and where I was going. I felt a renewed panic as I realized I was going to work for the same outfit and destination that she was.

We struck up a conversation to pass the time. She said that I looked familiar in an odd way, but she couldn't place me. She was practically glowing. She offered me a magazine, which I took without thinking. I concluded this must be her first time going out in the field. That kind of inner joy was hard to hold onto once you had been out there for a while.

I studied her. She seemed to be about 19, with blonde wavy hair and green eyes, wearing a taupe-colored dress with a laced V below her neckline. Stitched into the lace was the pattern of a vine with a single strawberry on it. She was holding a paperback in her lap, *By The Light Of the Moon*, a story I knew, written by the master, Dean Koontz.

The longer we talked, the more we found in common: music, movies, books, exploring, old cars, old movies. I made a passive note that there was no sign of a ring on her left hand.

I felt curious and concerned. For once, we were talking and my head wasn't spinning off its axis. But sorting out dream from reality was becoming an incredible challenge. I thought maybe she was just a face that I had seen before. Or maybe we would talk just long enough for me to once again try to warn her, and I would wake up in some other place and some other body.

She asked if I would like to grab a bite to eat when we landed. She said she knew a nice place near the airport.

My brain stalled. There was nothing I would rather do than

continue talking and getting to know this girl. And pictures began to flash through my mind: the restaurant and the little girl, the stage and the cafe, and the nurse on the floor with a blood stain on her dress in the shape of a strawberry.

Fumbling for the right words, I declined. "I am really sorry. I have to eat alone, or I have bad dreams. Long story, but I really appreciate the offer. There is almost nothing I would rather do."

I leaned back and closed my eyes. And I remembered the picture on the desk: the nurse and her husband and children. It came into focus, and I could see the man more clearly... it was me. And then it faded away.

I looked at the blank face of my phone, seeing the reflection of my 23-year-old self. I turned my head to face the window again, aiming my eyes to look at the billowing white cloud tops. The muscles around my throat contracted, and a single tear escaped my eye, drawing a tiny trail down my cheek.

ABOUT THE AUTHOR

Just a guy, who had an idea and a keyboard.

JJ Caler

MORE COFFEE AND DREAMS

Coffee and Dreams Volume 2
By
JJ Caler
Featuring Daniel Nick

Coffee and Dreams Volume 3
By
JJ Caler
Featuring J. Anne Brown, J
Lee Bagan and Daniel Nick

Coffee and Dreams Volume 4
By
JJ Caler
Featuring Arya Anakin, J Lee
Bagan and Daniel Nick

COFFEE AND DREAMS

VOLUME 2

SHORT STORIES WITH

JJ CALER

AND

Daniel Nick

COFFEE AND DREAMS
VOLUME 3
SHORT STORIES WITH
JJ CALER
J. Anne Brown - Daniel Nick - J Lee Bagan

COFFEE AND DREAMS
VOLUME 4
SHORT STORIES WITH
JJ CALER
Arya Anakin - Daniel Nick - J Lee Bagan

Jasper and the
Salamander
J. J. Caler

Erin
Rise
J. J. Caler

The Witch at the
World's End
J. J. Caler